ALICE'S
Wonderland
TEA PARTY

Poppy Bishop   *Laura Brenlla*

LITTLE TiGER

LONDON

Alice was having a tea party.
She had sent out perfect, neat invitations
and laid out delicate teacups.
"There," she said to Mad Hatter, "doesn't
that look just right?"

MORE TEA! MORE TEA!

I WONDER WHAT EVERYONE WILL BRING ...

"Oh dear! Oh dear! Am I late?" trembled White Rabbit, hopping up. "I've brought something sweet to eat."

"Clocks?" asked Alice. "Surely we can't eat those?"

"Of course we can!" scoffed Mad Hatter. "They taste delicious sprinkled with sugar . . .

. . . and dipped in tea!"

"Stop being silly!" cried Alice. "This is a proper tea party. I do hope someone brings something ORDINARY to eat."

Not a moment too soon, Dodo arrived.

"Salutations," he said. "I have brought a cake."

"Is it meant to be upside-down?" asked Alice, curiously. "How do we eat it?"

The right way up, they heard a rustling in the tree. It was Cheshire Cat with a pie. The pie certainly looked ordinary.

"Does it turn us upside-down?" asked Alice.

"Don't be ridiculous," said Cheshire Cat. "My pie . . .

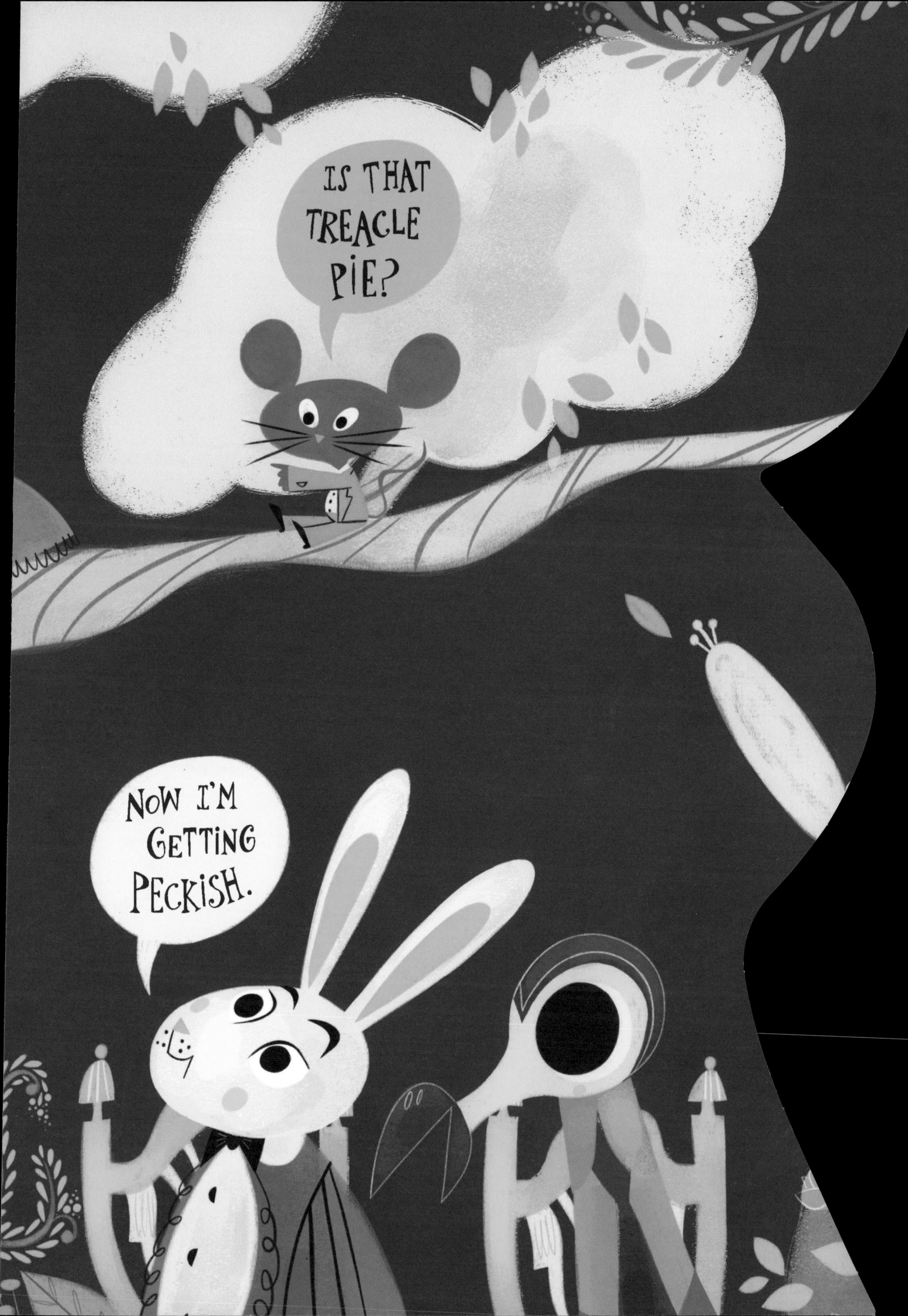
IS THAT TREACLE PIE?
NOW I'M GETTING PECKISH.

Just then a royal trumpet tooted and the Knave of Hearts strode in.

"Tarts for milady's tea party," he bowed.

"At last!" cheered Alice. "Something perfectly ordinary to eat."

"Oh NO," gulped the Mad Hatter, turning pale. "Don't eat THOSE! They belong to . . .

# of HEARTS!

"Those are MINE!" she bellowed.
"Off with their heads!"
And she snatched the tarts
(and the Knave of Hearts) and
took them clean away.

Everybody was starting to feel very hungry, when at last Cook and Duchess arrived.

"Hurrah! Eclairs!" cheered Alice.

"These eclairs," barked the Duchess, "are made with Cook's secret ingredient . . .

zzzzzzz

"Oh dear," sighed Alice. "This is the silliest
tea party ever."

Then she looked at her friends and
started to giggle. The tea party hadn't
been polite or perfectly proper,
but it had been FUN.

THERE'S
CAKE ON
MY HAT!

"Well," sighed Alice, "at last we have something normal to eat."

So they tidied the table and all sat down for a perfectly proper, TERRIBLY ordinary tea party . . .

"YOU started without ME!" huffed Caterpillar, wriggling up. "I'VE brought cupcakes."
  "Do they make us sneeze or disappear?" asked Alice.
  "No," said Caterpillar.
  "Oh," said Alice, a little disappointed.

. . . but not for long!

"Did I mention," said Caterpillar, "that my cupcakes are MAGIC!"

"Hurrah!" cheered Alice. "This really is the BEST TEA PARTY EVER!"